Silas

A Ghost Files Novella

By Apryl Baker

Silas

Limitless Publishing, LLC
Kailua, HI 96734
www.limitlesspublishing.com

Formatting: Limitless Publishing

ISBN-13: 978-1-64034-856-1
ISBN-10: 1-64034-856-5

Dedication

For all the Ghost Files Fans

Chapter One

Silas hummed to himself as he put his paints away. It had been a productive day. Two souls collected and one masterpiece finished.

The shouting from his studio pulled a sigh from him. As much as he enjoyed the company, he also enjoyed the quiet. Since his granddaughter came back into his life, quiet was something he ran short on.

He opened the door and looked out. Mattie's Hellhound was running back and forth like a possessed devil dog, and his granddaughter was trying to catch her. He wasn't sure if it was a game the two of them were playing or if the hound really had lost her mind.

Before he could say anything else, another Hellhound joined in. Damien howled and dived in after Peaches. His owner, Benny Malone, came rushing into the room. The child stopped and stared at the two big beasts tearing up the studio.

"Damien, no!"

Mattie looked up, startled, when she saw the boy. She didn't know Benny visited sometimes. Unfortunately, Silas had gotten caught up in collecting a soul and forgot to take the boy home before she arrived. He had a feeling she wouldn't like Benny spending time here. Silas was a demon, after all, and young Benny's family were hunters.

"Benny, what are you doing here?" She pushed her dark brown hair off her shoulder and dodged around the two Hellhounds.

"Visiting." The boy glanced over at Silas. "I missed him."

"You missed Silas?" Mattie's hazel eyes widened.

"Well, yeah. Don't you miss him

sometimes?"

Her gaze swung to Silas, and he closed the door to his soul room. "Do your parents know you're here?"

"Yup. They let me come for training."

"Training?"

"For Damien. Silas helps me with him. It's not easy having a Hellhound in your house all the time. Especially when others can't see him. Caleb stepped on his paw the other day, and I thought Damien was gonna chew his leg off."

"Huh. Peaches stays here a lot since I can't keep her at the dorm with me."

"It's good for the hound to be around other hounds. Gives him a sense of pack. And it allows him a place to get all that aggressive energy out. Hellhounds were never meant to be humans' pets."

"Silas, I don't know if I like Benny spending time here. Hellhound or not."

"I'm not going to harm the boy." Irritation flared. He was a demon, but he wasn't entirely evil. Even he had his limits. Besides, the boy had grown on him much the same way Mattie had.

"I know that." Her voice softened.

"I'm afraid of what he'll pick up. You…"

"Tend to forget I have a conscience and do horrible things?"

"I wasn't going to put it like that, but yes. He's a good kid. He doesn't need to lose his goodness."

"Uncle Silas doesn't do bad things around me," Benny said. "We play video games, watch football, and he's teaching me how to defend myself against monsters. Human *and* supernatural."

The boy had been taken by a pedophile inhabited by a Fallen Angel. Mattie refused to do anything to help Silas defeat Deleriel until Benny had been rescued. He'd found the child in the trunk of the car, tied up and bleeding from a head wound. He'd been fairly bruised as well.

His injuries could have come from rolling around in the trunk, but Silas didn't think so. Benny had been with the man for a few hours before Silas found him. The child wasn't raped. That much he was sure of, but everything else, well, that was a different story. Benny refused to talk about it with his therapist. Two years had gone by, and he still hadn't said anything. It wasn't a good situation. Silas took it upon himself to give the boy the tools to defend himself, should he find himself in that situation again. His hope was that during their training sessions, he could get the boy to talk.

"Uncle Silas?" Mattie arched a brow, a small smile playing on her lips.

Silas shrugged. "Are you two hungry? I was about to find dinner."

"Can we get chicken nuggets from McDonald's?" Benny's eyes got bright at the idea. "And chocolate milkshakes?"

"I could eat a Big Mac." Mattie's attention was drawn back to the mess the hounds were making. "Or three."

The girl could eat. How she packed that much food away was almost awe inspiring.

"You two clean this mess up, and I'll be back with food."

Silas shook his head as he walked toward the hallway outside his studio. McDonald's. Those two needed to learn to eat better.

Then again, he'd grown used to eating

junk food since these two spent so much time here. They were making him soft, but he didn't know how to stop it. Hell was going to take away his demon card if he couldn't figure out how to stop his conscience from growing a pair.

He hadn't even collected as many souls as he used to. In Hell, souls meant power. The more you had, the more powerful you were. He didn't tell the children that, though. They'd be horrified, and as much as he hated going soft, giving them up would be worse. They wouldn't visit, and he'd grown used to them. And their messes. And the noise they brought with them.

They were his family, and God or the Devil help anyone who dared to harm them.

When he returned from his trip to his least favorite fast food restaurant, his studio was on its way to being clean. At least all the furniture was picked up, but canvases and paper still littered the floor. Benny was sweeping and explaining to his Hellhound why he couldn't make messes. It was funny he thought the hound would listen to him. Hellhounds were notorious for making messes.

Mattie, however, was nowhere to be found. Frowning, he let his gaze wander over to his shelves of paint, thinking she might be bent down picking up brushes, but no.

What he did see alarmed him. The door to his soul room was open.

He dropped the bags and almost ran to the room. The girl needed to stay out of there. She was a living reaper, and her instinct was to save souls, not to trap them. He wouldn't put it past her to free every single one of them.

She was standing in the back corner of the room, looking at a jar he had set apart from the others. It was enclosed in a glass case with wards set up around it. He reserved that space for a special kind of soul. One who deserved all the pain and horror one could imagine inflicted upon them.

He'd only ever met one human who deserved the torment that cage brought on them.

"What are you doing, Emma Rose?"

He used her given name. She was Mattie to him, but she wanted to be called Emma. She had it in her head that her name was part of her past, a past she wanted to forget because of the pain those memories brought her.

She was slowly beginning to realize being Mattie Hathaway or Emma Crane was moot. They were the same person, and it didn't matter what she called herself.

"What is this?" she asked softly, her reaping abilities out in full force. He could smell it on her. It was like being in Antarctica. The snow had a distinctly salty smell, and that was what her reaping abilities smelled like to him. The frozen wasteland of snow and ice.

"Nothing for you to concern yourself with. The food's here. Let's eat before it gets cold."

She didn't budge. Her hand came up, and she rested it on the glass case. He saw the pain on her face when the wards activated, but she didn't remove her hand. She was getting stronger.

"Silas, what is this?"

"It's a soul protected by wards. If you don't move your hand soon, you're going to hurt later."

She snatched her hand back. "Why does it feel...so lost and helpless? And terrified? That came through more than any other emotion."

"Because that's how I want it to feel. What are you even doing in here, my darling girl? I thought you hated it."

"I do, but something kept calling to me, and I had to come see. It was this soul." Her gaze dropped back to the enclosure. "Why are you hurting it?"

"Because I can," he bit out. He didn't want to talk about that soul. "Besides, it's none of your business what I do with the souls I collect."

Her eyes narrowed. "No, it's not, but I'm making it my business. Why are you torturing that particular soul more than the others? The terror I can feel is almost crippling."

"It's none—"

"Of my business," Mattie finished for me. "Tough. I want to know what's going on here, Silas. This is wrong on so many levels, even for you."

"That soul deserves everything it's going through and more."

"Why? Who is it?"

"I don't want to talk about it."

She plopped down on the floor and leaned against the solid rock of the pedestal.

"I'm not moving until you talk."

"Do *not* make me hurt you, Mattie." He put a bit of a bite into his tone. She knew he hated hurting her, but she also knew he would if she made him.

Her hand cupped her cheek, remembering when he'd flayed the skin there. She understood better than anyone what he was capable of when he was angry or afraid.

"Silas, I can't ignore this. My reaping ability won't let me walk away from so much pain. I don't want you to hurt me, but I'll withstand it to get to the bottom of this."

"You don't understand."

"Make me understand."

"Hey!" Benny poked his head into the room. "The food is getting cold, and

Damien and Peaches are trying to eat it."

His eyes widened when he saw the racks and other torture devices in the room. "What is this place?" he whispered.

"See what you've done?" Silas accused. "The boy should never have seen this room. You went out of your way while you were both here to keep him out of here."

"Benny, go take the food to the dining room. Uncle Silas and I will be there in a few minutes."

"But…"

"No buts," Mattie said. "I'll tell you about this room, I promise, but first I need to talk to Uncle Silas."

"Okay."

She waited until he'd gone before crossing her arms over her chest and glaring. "Spill."

He arched a brow. "I am not a teenage girl."

"Silas."

"Mattie."

She frowned. He only used that name when he was particularly upset with her, and she knew that. He did not want to talk about the soul in that jar.

"Silas, who's in that jar? Will you at least tell me that?"

Why not? Maybe it would shock her into shutting up about the whole thing. "My sister."

Shock wasn't the right term for the expression on her face. He honestly couldn't describe it.

"Your sister," she said slowly. "The one I look like?"

"Yes."

"You created me to defeat Deleriel so you could rescue her soul. I don't understand, Silas. Why would you go through all that, put me through all that, when you're now torturing the woman you wanted to save?"

"I never said I wanted to rescue her, only that I wanted her soul."

"Silas, this is crazy. I…"

"You don't need to understand." He turned and walked out of the room. He hoped his granddaughter would stop with her inquisition, but he knew better. He only hoped she'd wait until the boy was gone.

He bypassed the dining room and went into his kitchen. While he technically didn't have to eat, he enjoyed food and partook of it quite often. His kitchen had all the various equipment one would expect and a cozy table that could seat four. He found Benny there instead of the dining room. He'd put the food on the small breakfast table.

"Ben, can you get us drinks out of the fridge?"

The boy nodded, but he was quiet. He'd seen the torture devices in the room. Silas had tried to keep him out of there, and it seemed fate was not on his side. The boy shouldn't be down here in the first place. He was human, and humans didn't do well around demons. Or Hell in general.

Mattie walked in, her expression troubled. "Silas, you need to explain this to me."

"Not now, my darling girl. Let's eat, get young Ben home, and then maybe we'll talk about the jar."

"Uncle Silas, why did you have all that

stuff in there?"

It was twenty questions today with these two.

"That room is not something you should have seen."

"But I did see it."

"He's not going to forget about it," Mattie said as she sat down at the table. "You might as well tell him what it is."

If he did that, Ben might tell his parents, and he wouldn't be able to come back. Or he might decide not to come back himself after hearing what that room was for, two possibilities Silas was not looking forward to. The boy meant something to him.

Mattie and Ben were his two weaknesses. He'd loved his granddaughter from the day he'd held her. When he lost her, it had nearly killed him. And then Benny came along. The boy had wormed himself into Silas's heart without even trying.

It would break him to lose them.

That was something he kept hidden from everyone. He had to appear strong and without weaknesses to all the other

14

demons. If they found out about either of these two, they'd use them against him.

And he couldn't have that.

Perhaps it was better for them to finally cut him out. It would solve so many problems. But could he give them up? He wasn't sure.

"It's my room of souls."

The boy's eyes widened.

"I'm a demon, Benny. I make deals all day long for souls. Humans are weak, and they want things they shouldn't have. When that happens, they call upon us to give them what their hearts desire. We do, and in exchange, we collect their souls. That room holds all the souls I've collected over the centuries."

"Souls equal power in Hell, don't they?"

He was surprised the boy knew that, but he supposed he shouldn't be. He was the son of James Malone, one of the best hunters in the business. James knew more about the supernatural than most.

"Yes, they do."

"Do you have a lot of them?"

Silas smiled and started passing out

food. "Of course. How do you think I can have all this?"

Benny took his chicken nuggets and chocolate milkshake. "But why are there…those things in there?"

"Sometimes a soul wants to renege on their deal. When that happens, they have to be taught a lesson. Those devices help me to teach them their place."

"You hurt them?" His aqua colored eyes were wide, and a new kind of horror filled them.

"Yes, Benjamin, I hurt them. I'm a demon. You must remember that. I'm not a good person. I'm evil."

"But you *are* a good person." Benny opened his nuggets. "Even good people do bad things." His eyes swung to Mattie. "Like what you had to do in that room when we were here before. You did bad things so you could kill Deleriel."

Mattie nodded. Silas often wondered how she'd reconciled herself with the things she'd done to prepare for her fight with Deleriel. His granddaughter was a special person. She had a soul unlike any he'd ever seen. He'd harmed that soul when he forced her to torture souls, but it was necessary. She'd never have survived if he hadn't done that.

"Benny, that room is necessary for me, but I understand if you don't want to come back here."

"No, it's cool. That room is important for you, and what you do in there is your business, not mine."

The boy's acceptance of that surprised him, though. He seemed willing to forgive what went on in there. Silas didn't understand.

"I..." He cleared his throat. "Let's eat before this gets cold."

"It's already cold." Mattie took a drink from her Coca-Cola can. It was her second favorite drink, after orange juice. "Now, about your sister's soul. Why is it locked in a torture chamber?"

"You locked your sister in a torture chamber?" Benny's eyes widened so much they were almost too big for his face.

Silas sighed. He did not want to do this, but he couldn't take the accusation in the boy's eyes. Ben understood evil better than most, but loving his sister the way he did, he might not be so forgiving of this particular evil.

"Neither of you is going to let this go, are you?"

They both shook their heads.

"Fine, I'll tell you, but if you judge me, keep it to yourselves."

And so Silas began the tale he hoped never to tell.

Chapter Two

Silas David Haversham, future Duke of Kent, stopped his horse in front of his home where Keith, the stable boy, waited patiently to take the animal.

"Rub him down well. He's been put through his paces today."

"Yes, milord." The boy nodded and took the reins of his horse, Stormborne. The child looked too young to be working. He'd have to speak with the child's father. He did not like children working when they were not old enough. Accidents happened. Two children died last year on the property adjacent to Silas's. They were both under ten.

He strode through the double doors of his family's country home and called out for his wife, Celia. He'd been worried about her recently. She was heavy with child, and she seemed more tired with this one than she had with their daughter, Mathilda.

"Papa!" The girl came flying down the stairs and threw herself at him, her blonde hair flying in all directions. "I missed you!"

"Were you good for your mother while I was away?"

Her blue eyes, her mother's eyes, wouldn't meet his.

"Mathilda Rose, look at your father."

She looked up, and he knew she'd misbehaved.

"You know your mother is not well, and you were supposed to be a good girl while I was gone."

"I wanted to see the piggies," she said, her face set in her I'm-about-to-cry expression. "They were in town, and the babies were so cute."

For a girl of five, she was as rambunctious as a boy of ten. She should have been a boy, he thought, she since she behaved more like one.

"Aunty Serene took me to see them. She thought they were cute too."

Ah, of course. His sister never minded her father either. Or him, for that matter. She did what she wanted when she wanted, much like the child in his arms.

"Finish your story."

"Mother said I wasn't supposed to get dirty since we were out in public."

"And?" Silas prompted when the girl didn't say anything else.

"And she climbed the fence and got down in the mud with all the pigs. She proceeded to chase them until she caught one."

He looked to see his wife standing at the top of the stairs, her blonde hair piled on top of her head in an intricate design. The blue dress she wore made her eyes stand out. She was just as beautiful today as the day he'd married her six years ago. His desire for her had not waned either.

"Mathilda Rose Haversham, what did I say?"

"I was supposed to be a good girl and

mind Mother," she whispered.

"I brought you home a surprise, but you will not receive it today. You will think about what you did tonight instead. Am I understood?"

"Yes, Papa." She laid her head on his shoulder, and he gave in and kissed her forehead.

"Papa loves you, but you must learn to behave."

She nodded and sniffed. He put her down and turned to his wife, who had made her way down the stairs.

Celia came willingly into his arms, and he kissed her with all the pent-up desire he'd suffered through during the last week.

"Did you have a good trip into London, my love?" Celia smiled up at him, and his heart constricted. He'd never loved a woman like he did her. His child came first, but Celia meant just as much to him. He loved her.

"I did. The king approved our expansion into the New World. Father will be pleased."

"Your father had an episode while you

were away."

"How bad was it?"

"The physician said it was his heart and confined him to his bed. As you can imagine, he's not taking it well."

"He's been saying bad words," Mathilda piped in. "I laughed, but Mother says I'm not to say those words or laugh at Grandfather when he's ill."

"Your mother is absolutely right." Secretly, he agreed with his daughter. His father's behavior probably bordered on being funny. He hated being confined to his bed and could get rather hostile about it.

"It's time for your bath, young lady. Go find Janey. She's waiting for you."

"Yes, Mother." The girl scuffed her pink shoe against the floor, and Silas reached down and picked her up. He kissed both her cheeks and then her forehead. "Papa loves you, my darling girl."

"I love you too, Papa." Her face broke out into a smile. "You're not mad?"

"No, I'm not mad, but you still do not get your surprise until tomorrow. Now, go get your bath before the water gets cold." He put her down, and she scampered up the stairs with the same vigor as she had come down them.

Celia laughed at her antics. "That girl. She takes after your sister."

"I hope not. One Serene is enough."

"That is the God's truth if there ever was one." Celia rubbed her belly, her face tired.

"How are you feeling?" Silas wrapped an arm around her and escorted her into the sitting room. She'd decorated it in tones of blue and gold. His father had agreed to let her redecorate, but he'd watched her like a hawk, thinking Celia would want to do everything in shades of pink. Yes, she wore a lot of pink, but she understood her favorite color would not go over well with everyone and instead used neutral tones to redesign the manor house. Even his father had to admit it turned out well.

"Tired, but it's almost time for you to meet our son."

They sat, and he asked one of the servants to bring them something cold to drink. The heat seemed unbearable this year.

"I'll be perfectly fine if the babe is another girl. It might give Mathilda a reason to calm down if she helps to take care of her little sister and we tell her she must set the example for the girl."

Celia laughed so hard she snorted. "You honestly think our Mathilda would be a good example for the little one? She would drag the child off into the mud to chase piglets alongside her."

"I was hoping the new baby would help to settle her."

"No, my love, she's not going to be too happy when the baby gets all the attention. She's going to act out."

"And you know this how?"

"Because that is what I did when my sister was born."

"I doubt that." He thanked the servant for their drinks and made sure Celia drank hers. "You do not look well."

"This one seems to enjoy making me sick day and night. He and I are going to have a talk about that when he comes into the world. I have a feeling he's going to be as much trouble as our darling girl."

"No one could be that much trouble." Silas set his drink down. "I should go see Father. He must be in an unbearable mood."

"He is." Celia wrinkled her nose. "He even refused to eat this morning. He says he is dying and to let him."

"He will outlive us all. Of that, I am certain." Silas kissed his wife and stood. "Wish me luck."

Chapter Three

The Duke of Kent, Douglas Ezekiel Haversham, was sitting up in bed, his back resting against a mountain of pillows. His expression was pinched, and Silas knew without anyone telling him that his father was not well. He could see it in the lines of his face. He was pale, and sweat beaded his brow. It might have been from the heat, but Silas doubted it.

"Hello, Father." Silas opened the drapes and let in the late afternoon sunlight. The chamber looked like a death room, and he wasn't having it.

"Leave them closed, boy, and let me die in peace." His voice shook when he spoke, and real fear gripped Silas. He'd never heard his father's voice do that before. This last episode with his heart may have done some serious damage.

"Old man, get yourself out of your grouchy mood. You are about to meet your grandson any day now."

"Bah. Boy or girl, it doesn't matter when Mathilda is as much a boy as she is a girl. I wouldn't trade her for ten grandsons."

Silas smiled. His daughter had her grandfather wrapped around her finger. All she had to do was pout, and he'd give her the world.

"Either way, your grandson will be here any day, and he'll expect a doting grandfather. And what will Mathilda think if you give up on life and allow yourself to die? What will that teach her? A little hardship, and you give up?"

"That girl has more grit in her than any of us. She's fearless."

"That's true, Father, but she watches and learns. Would you have her learn to give up because of an illness, should she get sick?"

Silas knew playing on his father's love for Mathilda was wrong, but he'd do anything to get him out of this state of mind, given how ill he looked.

The old man made a noise and sat up further. "Where is our darling girl?"

"Getting a bath."

"Did she tell you about her escapades in town with the pigs?" Douglas laughed, but it ended on a wheeze, which worried Silas even more.

"She did. I told her she had to wait until tomorrow for her surprise since she disobeyed her mother and got dirty."

"Dirty doesn't do it justice. She came home covered in mud. I couldn't even tell it was her. The carriage had to be cleaned. It took her nurse a good hour of scrubbing before she started to look like a little girl again. The child should have been a boy."

Silas didn't disagree. "My audience with the King went well. He approved our plans to expand into the New World, and he gave us the funding needed to do so."

"I am surprised. He's been frugal with

who he is allowing to travel there, especially after the Roanoke fiasco."

"Jamestown has been successful, Father. I think it would do our family good to get away from London and start over in the New World."

"You want to go yourself?" Douglas looked up, surprised. "I thought you were sending over representatives for our shipping company to expand into trading there."

"I have thought long and hard on this, Father. Benjamin and I spoke long into the night on this just a fortnight ago. London has grown crowded and so political it has become an issue to say a greeting for fear of reprisal from the King's court. Those people are brutal. I do not want my children growing up in that environment. In the New World, they'll learn values and what it means to work hard for the results you want. My son will not be raised in a political environment."

Douglas nodded, his expression thoughtful. "I do not think I'll make the trip, so all I ask is that you put off the trip until I pass."

Silas did not want to think of a world without his father, but looking at the old man, he knew as well as his father did, the old man didn't have much time left. He should be able to spend that time with his family.

"We have to talk about your sister."

That got Silas's attention. His father sounded serious. "I know she was the instigator behind my daughter's adventures in town. I plan on speaking with her about it. We must not cause Celia any stress. She does not look well."

"No, it is not that. I have managed to scare away all her suitors, save one. He has been rather persistent."

"Who?"

"Lord Brewer. He recently became an earl when his father died aboard ship in a sudden storm at sea. He has taken a shine to our Serene and asked for her hand in marriage."

"What does Serene say?"

"She seems as taken with him as he is with her."

"I hear suspicion in your voice, Father.

Do you have reason to doubt his admiration of our Serene?"

"There is something about the man that does not sit well with me. I cannot tell you why, but perhaps when you meet him, you will understand my caution."

"I will speak with Serene about him. Perhaps we should invite him to dinner since I have returned home?"

Douglas nodded. "Yes, I'll send an invitation to him to come tomorrow night. I know he's due home from London today. He had to visit his solicitor to take care of some business left over from his father's death."

"How long ago did he ask for her hand?"

"The day he went to London. I told him I would consider his request while he was gone."

"And after a week, you still do not know?"

"No. I am not sure we should entrust Serene into his care."

"No decisions have to be made today. I will speak with Serene and get a read on the man when he comes to dinner tomorrow night. We will get to the bottom of your caution, Father."

"Good. Now leave me be. I am tired and must rest."

"Of course, Father."

Silas only hoped playing on his father's love for Mathilda would give the old man the strength to fight. He was not ready to lose his father.

Chapter Four

He knocked on his sister's door and opened it. Neither of them ever waited for the other to reply. They simply waltzed in. Since he'd married Celia, Serene at least called out before she entered his bedchamber. So far, there had been no embarrassing moments for Celia. He hoped that held true until the girl was married and settled in her own home.

Serene was sitting in a chair by the window overlooking the gardens. She and Silas looked very much alike with their dark hair. She had their mother's hazel eyes, though. He could understand why she had so many suitors. She'd grown into a beautiful young woman. It would take a strong man to handle her, but he would have to do so with a gentle hand. Silas would not give his sister to someone who would mistreat her because of her wild nature and inability to listen to anyone but herself.

"I hear you had my daughter running rampant in a pigpen."

She looked up from her book and smiled. "You're home, brother." She tossed the book aside and rushed him in much the same manner as Mathilda had. "It is good to have you home. Father's illness has scared me to my bones."

"He does not look well," Silas agreed and kissed his sister on the forehead. "I think I managed to at least remove him from his deathbed. I reminded him that my daughter learns from us all."

"He loves her more than he does us," Serene said ruefully. "Now, what did you bring me?"

"Who says I brought you anything, imp?"

"You always bring me things from your trips."

"Perhaps I should withhold your gift as I did Mathilda's for disobeying her mother. You were the instigator of it."

"I had no idea she would climb the fence like a little monkey." Serene grinned at the memory, and Silas found himself grinning along with her, imagining his daughter scaling the fence and showing her underthings to the entire world. "I just wanted her to see the baby pigs, not get into the pen and chase them."

"My wife informs me she caught one."

"She did and promptly demanded to bring it home with her for a pet."

"Good Lord, she did not."

"She did, but Celia was adamant. She was not allowing a pig into her home to run rampant."

"Only my daughter," Silas muttered fondly.

"So, as you can see, I instigated nothing. I was merely showing the girl the piglets. They looked adorable. Now, where is my gift?"

Silas reached into his pocket and pulled out a small package. He had found a beautiful opal ring he knew his sister would adore. He handed it over, and she promptly ripped the packaging off. Serene was never one to gently remove the wrapping from any gift. She squealed when she saw the ring and slid it onto her finger.

"It's beautiful, Silas! Thank you!" She gave him a hug so tight, it almost cut off his breathing, but that was his sister. She never did anything halfway.

"I am glad you like it. Come sit with me. Father tells me you have gone and gotten yourself a suitor he cannot chase off."

Her grin turned into a soft, shy smile, which told him how much she liked the gentleman. "Lord Brewer is the kindest man, Silas. He sees my wildness as part of me and does not want to change me. All the others told Father they would be able to get me under control within a month. Father chased them all away. Except for Lord Brewer. I do not know why Father is so hesitant to allow the marriage. I approve, and I think you will too once you meet Evan."

"It is Evan, is it?" Silas teased and watched the blush crawl up his sister's face. She hardly ever blushed. She truly was smitten with the man. "Father says he is being cautious, as well he should. He is your father, and giving his only daughter to anyone should be something he thinks over carefully. He does not want you to end up in a bad marriage."

"I understand that, Silas. Truly, I do. I just hope Father doesn't let his own caution cost me a marriage where I can be happy."

"I promise I will not let that happen, poppet. I will interview your young man tomorrow night, and if he passes my inquisition, then I will persuade Father to allow the marriage."

"Inquisition?" Her eyes widened. "You won't scare him off, will you, Silas? I...I think I may love him."

"You think?" Silas smiled indulgently. Serene was but sixteen. He was not sure she even understood the love between a woman and a man. He had known he loved Celia the first time he laid eyes upon her at a Christmas ball. She, however, had not wanted anything to do with him. He had been a wild one in his early days. Her father, however, thought differently. Silas's father was cousin to the King, and a marriage between Silas and Celia would raise Celia's family status at court. It had taken him months to get her to come around to his way of thinking, and she allowed herself to fall in love with him as hard as he had fallen for her.

His eyes landed on the book she'd been reading, and he picked it up. *The Art of the Mystics*. He opened the book and looked through it. "Why are you reading such nonsense, Serene?"

She snatched it away from him. "I find it interesting."

"It is blasphemy, Serene. If anyone catches you with this, they could accuse you of witchcraft."

"It is not witchcraft, Silas." She clutched the book to her. "It is simply the ways of another culture. It is interesting to me."

He pried the book from her. She held on tight, but he was stronger. "You will not read anything like this ever again, Serene. I will not have my sister accused of witchcraft. Imagine if one of the servants found this and went crying to the priest. Even having this in your room is enough to cause them to accuse you."

"I…I am sorry, Silas. I did not think of the risk. I will not read anything of this nature again."

"Swear it to me, Serene."

She looked him in the eyes. "I swear."

"Good girl." He kissed her forehead. "I'll see you at dinner."

Silas left his sister's room, making sure the title of the book was hidden as he made his way to his father's study where he tossed the book in the fireplace and started a fire himself.

What was the girl thinking?

Shaking his head, he stayed there until the last page had burned.

Chapter Five

Evan Brewer, the Earl of Ducanth, was a tall man, broad in the shoulder, with long legs and a lean waist. Silas could not gauge his age, though. He had one of those faces. He could have been twenty-five or forty-five. Silas made a note to find out. He refused to allow his sister to marry a man old enough to be her father. It occurred more than he cared to admit in the aristocracy, but Serene would not fall victim to that particular age-old tradition.

"Now, now, my love, get that predatory look off your face." Celia slid her arm through his and handed him a brandy. "You cannot scare him away before giving him a chance."

Silas snorted. "If he runs that easily, he will never be able to keep up with our poppet."

"Silas."

He heard the warning in his wife's voice and chose to ignore it. "Would you want me to do any less for our daughter than I would for my own sister?"

That hushed her. As well it should have. She knew how much he loved his sister and that he would do anything to protect her. Even from herself and her own feelings.

Silas pulled his wife close, and together, they walked to where Lord Brewer stood speaking with his father, who had pulled himself from his deathbed. He still looked unwell, but his color was perhaps a bit better tonight. Or it could have been the glow of the firelight giving him an appearance of improved health.

"Lord Brewer, I want to thank you for accepting our invitation to dinner tonight." Celia broke away from Silas and did her best impression of a curtsy. With their birth of their son imminent, it proved a little difficult.

"Please, my lady, do not overexert yourself on my account." Lord Brewer's voice was rich and cultured. He extended his arm and led her to the seat next to Serene. "Here, sit."

Of course, Celia smiled up at him. Silas had to admit he cut a rather dashing figure with his blond hair and blue eyes. He seemed almost too perfect. Granted, it was his job to be suspicious of the fellow, but his father was right. There was something about the man that did not sit well with Silas. And for the life of him, he couldn't put it into words. It was right there on the tip of his tongue.

"Tell us, Lord Brewer, what is it you do? I am unfamiliar with your family." Silas again ignored the rebuke in both females' expressions. He was doing his family duty here, and they were not going to make him shirk it.

"I am not surprised." The man smiled and leaned against the hearth. "My father was never one for court, and Mother was always ill. He preferred to keep watch over her while I grew up. I was tutored at home because of it. I've spent a great deal of time in Spain since coming of age, however. We do a good bit of business in importing and exporting."

"You own your own shipyards?" Strange, Silas had never heard of them, if that was the case, and he would have. The Havershams owned the largest shipyard in London.

"No. We tend to deal with the smaller shippers and lessen our expense."

Silas's eyes narrowed. He knew every ship owner in London. Most of them had come to him at one point or another for help with something, even something as small as sails for their masts. Silas prided himself on having the best of the best. He didn't overcharge either, something that was appreciated by those not able to afford the massive trade ships he was known for.

"Really? With whom have you done business? Perhaps I know them."

Something shifted behind the man's eyes. It was there and gone so fast, had

Silas not been watching, he wouldn't have seen it.

"The Gages and I do regular business. They are honorable in their dealings with my family, and we repay that honor by staying loyal to them."

The answer sounded truthful, but Silas made a mental note to check the man's story.

"I know Henry Gage. He's a good man. Buys his sails from me."

Again, something slid behind Brewer's eyes. It unnerved Silas more than anything else. It was like there was someone else in there listening, but that made no sense.

"Well, I am certain he will give me a good reference."

"Let us hope so." Silas grinned the same grin that had gotten him and Benjamin St. Germaine, his best friend since childhood, into more trouble than he could easily get out of. It thrilled the ladies and terrified the men.

Lord Brewer only smiled in return.

The housekeeper announced dinner was ready, and his wife used the opportunity to scold him as they made their way into the dining room. He was not to be deterred, though. Something was wrong here, and he would find out what it was.

"Behave," she whispered before allowing him to seat her.

There was a commotion in the hallway, and Benjamin strode in, looking as rakish as ever with his chestnut hair and unusual aqua eyes. He'd stolen more than one kiss on just those eyes alone.

"Sorry for the late arrival. It couldn't be helped. My mistress decided I wasn't allowed out of the house until she was done with me." He grinned and winked at the women.

Both were used to him, but Brewer was not. He gasped and started to say something, but Silas held up a hand. "No need to take him to task for his crude language around the ladies. It won't do you a bit of good."

"He's harmless," Serene said.

Benjamin put a hand to his heart. "You wound me, my beauty. I'm far from harmless."

Serene giggled, and Brewer glanced at her. He did not look happy. Which was precisely why Silas had asked his friend to dinner. He knew Serene had a schoolgirl crush on Benjamin and hoped to see if that was all she felt for Brewer. In turn, he'd told Benjamin about his father's suspicions when it came to the man, and Benjamin agreed to help suss out if Brewer's intentions were honest or if he was looking to attach himself to a relative of the king.

"Boys, I'm starved. Quit your teasing until after I've had my fill." Douglas sat down at the head of the table and signaled to the servants to begin serving the first course.

"Brewer is in exporting," Silas told his friend as he sat beside him.

"Really?" Benjamin looked over at the man with interest. "I do quite a bit myself. I import and export fine wines."

"We do a lot of grain exporting. Mainly to Spain."

"I have several contacts in Spain. We'll have to compare notes. Now, when did you meet our lovely Serene? I know

I've been to all the same balls she has attended. I chaperoned her at several when her father and Silas couldn't take her."

"We didn't meet at a ball." Evan took a sip of wine. "As I told Lord Haversham, I was not brought up around the court and did not attend any of the parties, even here in the country. My father abhorred them. I met Serene in town while I was there to see about some goods Father was interested in. I saw her in the market and had to introduce myself."

"Hmmm." Silas watched Benjamin's reaction and noted he seemed suspicious of Brewer too. Really, who had never attended a party in all their life? Boys would be boys and snuck out while their fathers thought them all tucked away. It was simply the way of boys.

And girls. His own Mathilda had snuck out of her room on more than one occasion, and she was but five years of age. A grown man couldn't say he'd never done the same. Preposterous.

"I…" Celia leaned over and clutched her belly.

"What is it? What's wrong?" Silas was instantly on alert.

"I think your son has decided he wants to meet you." Her smile was watery, and she was clearly in pain.

"How long has this been going on?" he demanded. He knew from the birth of his daughter, a woman's labor could linger for hours. This type of pain was typical of the later stages.

"Just a few minutes, but…" Again, she cried out. "I think something is wrong."

Silas felt the blood leach from his face. "Benj, fetch the physician. Serene, tell the servants to find Mrs. Roth. She'll know what to do." Silas stood and lifted his wife into his arms and all but ran, taking the stairs two at a time.

He felt the wetness of her tears against his neck as they entered their bedchamber. It tore him apart when she cried or was in pain and there was nothing he could do.

Mrs. Ross bustled in and tried to shoo him out of the room. She should have known better. He'd sat by Celia's side when she had labored through the birth of their daughter, and he'd sit by her side through this one as well. Boy or girl, he didn't care. He just hoped the child came quicker than Mathilda. She'd put her mother through fourteen hours of labor.

"Help me get her changed," Mrs. Ross, the housekeeper and midwife for all the ladies in the area, ordered him. She handed him a nightdress, and he told Celia to sit down so he could help her out of her gown. But the sight of the red stain on her dress paralyzed him. Mrs. Ross turned and saw it too. Worry entered her eyes.

Silas kept his concern to himself and stripped his wife down. Blood ran in rivers down her thighs. This was not normal.

"Silas?" Celia was staring wide-eyed at the blood. "Silas, I…" She swayed, and he caught her before she fell.

"This is not good, my lord." Mrs. Ross helped him get her into bed, not bothering with the nightgown. She ordered him across the room while she examined her. She came back a moment later. "I cannot stop the bleeding, milord.

There's nothing I can do for her or the babe. I'm sorry."

"No," Silas whispered. "I cannot lose her."

Just minutes ago, she'd been laughing and scolding him. How had this happened? How had she gone from that to all the life's blood pouring out of her?

"I am so sorry. The best thing you can do for her now is to be with her in these last moments."

His hands shook, but he knew Mrs. Roth was right. He would not leave her to die alone and in pain, even if that was how she would leave him. Her face was pale, even in the candlelight.

"I'm sorry, my love," she whispered, her voice strained.

"Do not be sorry, Celia." Tears ran down his face as he watched the life start to slip from her. Mrs. Roth quietly left the room. "I'm here with you, and I love you." He pulled her close and held her.

Benj burst into the room, and his gaze went directly to Silas quietly sobbing. He closed the door and came to stand by the bed. Silas did not tell him to go, as Benj had been with him through everything. He wouldn't let Silas spiral down into helplessness, even if he wanted to.

"Do you remember when we were boys and we went into the room at the top of the stairs Father kept locked?"

Silas looked up at his best friend, confused. Why was he bringing that up now?

"Do you remember the strange things we saw in that room and how Father nearly beat us black and blue for daring to go in there?"

"Yes."

"The things in that room were artifacts that were cursed, things he and men like him protected the world from. I fear that is what is happening here."

"What are you saying?"

"This…this is too sudden. Something caused this. I cannot save your wife. She is gone, but I can save the babe if you let me."

"I…" Silas looked down at his wife. She'd stopped breathing. "How?"

"Do you trust me?"

"With my life."

"Then move, Silas, and let me help your son."

Silas moved. As much as he loved Celia, he loved his children more, even one he had not met.

He watched as Benj pulled out a long dagger, one Silas knew from experience was sharper than any blade he'd ever run across, and turned to Celia's lifeless body. Silas turned away, unable to watch as his best friend butchered his wife to get to the child that rested inside her. A cry cut through the air a moment later, and as grief-stricken as he was, relief played a part in that grief.

He ran to the door and called for Mrs. Roth. The woman was already hurrying down the hall, having heard the baby's cry. She came into the room, wide-eyed. "What have you done?"

"Saved the child. I just regret I could not do the same for his mother." Benj handed the babe to her. "You have a son, Silas."

A boy. Celia promised him a son, and a son she had given him.

But at what cost?

His shoulders sagged as his grief overwhelmed him.

"Come, Silas. Let us go downstairs. You need to be with family."

Silas's world went fuzzy, and he didn't really remember anything at all after that.

Chapter Six

It had been a fortnight since he'd lost Celia. Mathilda didn't understand any more than he did. She constantly cried for her mother, and he did the same where no one could see. The days blurred around him, but that could be due to the fact he stayed drunk most of the time.

Benj had finally grown fed up with his drunkenness, reminding Silas he had two children who needed him, two children who were suffering just as much as he from the loss of their mother. He'd been here all day, refusing to let Silas drink anything but tea and water. His stomach rebelled after its two-week-long binge on nothing save alcohol.

He didn't want to be sober, no matter how true Benj's words rang. He didn't want to face the world without Celia.

It had been his daughter who crawled into his lap and asked him if he was going to go away like her mother had. She looked so scared and lost, it pierced his own cloud of grief. No matter how much pain he was in, he was at least old enough to understand death. His five-year-old was not.

She was the reason he was sitting in the rocking chair in her room watching her sleep. Her blonde hair was matted around her head from all the tossing and turning she was doing. Her thumb was stuck firmly in her mouth, something she hadn't done since she was two. They almost never broke her of that habit, but her nurse assured them it would cause problems with her teeth later.

There was a knock at the door, and Benj came in, the baby in his arms. "I thought it high time you met your son. He still doesn't have a name."

Silas had avoided the baby like the

plague. Part of him blamed the child for Celia's death. It wasn't true, but the irrational part of him did, all the same. He was afraid he couldn't love the boy because of it.

"He looks like you, but he has his mother's eyes." Benj came over and thrust the baby at him.

Silas gripped the child for fear of him falling, but he didn't look at him. He couldn't.

"Is this what Celia would have wanted?" Benj demanded. "She loved that boy from the moment she knew she carried him. Would she want you to shirk him? If she could see you now, she'd slap you and demand you care for your child."

"Papa?" Mathilda's soft voice interrupted them. She sat up in bed, rubbing her eyes. "Is Mother home yet?"

And his heart broke all over again. "No, my darling girl. Mother isn't coming home. She's gone to Heaven."

"But I want her to come home."

"So do I, sweetheart, but she cannot. We are all that we have left, and we have to be brave for each other."

The girl climbed out of bed and into his lap, snuggling into him. "I miss her."

"I do too." He used his free hand to stroke her hair. She was an exact replica of Celia, and as much as it hurt him to look at her, it helped him too. He loved his child more than he loved himself. "Papa is sorry he has been so distant."

"It is all right, Papa." She leaned up and kissed his cheek. "I am sad too."

Benj smiled softly. "How about we name your son? The child will think his name is Baby if we do not."

"Can we call him Rupert?" Mathilda's eyes were bright when she looked up at him, some of the pain diminishing with excitement over naming her baby brother.

"Rupert?" He cocked a brow in question.

"I like it."

"I do not think you brother will, though, when he gets older." He gathered his courage and looked down at his son, who was watching him with avid curiosity. His blue eyes were intelligent and so like his mother's, even at this age, it took his breath away. The same love he had for his daughter swelled up inside. This was his child, his son. He had not been fair to the babe, blaming him for his mother's death. Benj was right. Celia would have slapped him. No, Celia would have had Benj knock some sense into him. She had done it on more than one occasion over the years.

"He will!" Mathilda declared.

Benj turned away to hide his laughter at the child's determination that her brother would adore a vile name. Rupert. Where did she get her ideas?

"Well, I think Benjamin Douglas Haversham is a good name. After all, it was your Uncle Benj who saved his life."

"He did?" Mathilda asked, her gaze swinging to her uncle, who looked a little wet around the eyes.

"Yes. He knew what to do to save him. For that, I am eternally grateful."

"See here, now, do not be expecting me to name my firstborn son after you." Ben smiled and came to stand by the rocking chair. "To be fair, Benjamin is a far better name than Silas. I always manage to get the girls."

Silas laughed. "Come, now, my darling girl, let Uncle Benj put you back to bed. He shall even tell you a story."

"I will?"

"You will." Silas nodded, and Mathilda scampered off his lap and ran to her bed. She loved her uncle's stories. He told her outrageous tales of pirates and damsels in distress.

While Benj did that, Silas got up and went downstairs, his son held tightly against him. He wanted a few minutes alone with the boy. His father's library provided that, so he sat in one of the two chairs in front of the fireplace. He always loved it in here. They were fortunate enough to have a large collection of books. It was a luxury many could not afford, but their business granted it to them.

The baby made a sound, and he looked down, alarmed, terrified he had held him too close or perhaps too tightly, but that was not the case. The child blinked and made the noise again. Silas realized he was just making normal baby sounds. He laid the child in his lap and traced the outline of his face. He did look like him. Benj was right. The shape of his eyes, however, that was all Celia. He hoped little Ben kept the blue color of his eyes.

"I am very sorry I have ignored you, little one. I was so sad about your mother, I couldn't breathe through the pain. It wasn't only you I ignored, but your sister too. Neither of you deserved that, especially you. You never got to meet your mother, and you'll never know how much she adored you. But I will tell you about her and remind you every day how much she loved you."

The fire crackled as he and his son sat quietly staring at each other. His father once told him he would understand the depths a person would go to in order to protect those he loved once he held his child in his arms. His father had been right. There was no bond like that between a parent and a child. He grieved his wife deeply, but should he lose either of his children, it would devastate him. Should someone harm his child, may God help them. There would be no place they could hide from him.

For the first time since Celia died, some of the grief eased the tiniest bit, and he owed that to his children.

He would protect them and love them enough for both himself and Celia.

Chapter Seven

A month after Celia died, Silas lost his father. He had another episode with his heart, and it was one he wasn't able to rebound from. It hurt. The pain of losing his wife and his father so close together almost crippled him, but his children kept him centered in the here and now. They needed their father, especially Mathilda. The child loved her grandfather as much as she did Silas. She cried for days, and Silas carried her. He very rarely put her down that first week after Douglas's death. It was not fair that a child should have to lose so much so quickly. It bruised her soul. That was what Benj said. He told Silas to keep her close.

The look on his face when he'd said it worried Silas so much, he let the child sleep in his bed at night. He'd even had the baby's cradle moved into his room. The nurse slept in the sitting room his wife had kept in their chambers. His sister thought he was being ridiculous, but a man knew when something was wrong.

His memories of the night his wife died had been fuzzy, but the more he thought about Benj's odd expression, the more that night came back to him. Specifically, what Benj had told him. He'd thought what happened to Celia was unnatural. He'd asked Silas if he remembered going into the locked room at Benj's country house and how his father had nearly skinned them alive for doing it. It was a lesson neither of them forgot growing up. They steered clear of that room.

He remembered it had been filled with old statues, books, trinkets, and even a few things he had no words to describe. It scared him back then, and it still scared him today. Silas knew Benj did not practice witchcraft, but he'd often wondered if Benj's father had. Was that why he'd been so forceful in not only his words, but his actions in keeping the two of them out of that room?

It was these thoughts that drove him to find his friend, who was down at the stables looking over a horse that had fallen ill. The mare was barely two and had been in prime health only a week ago, but according to the stable boy, he'd found the mare lying down in her stall, and she couldn't be coaxed to stand.

Which was what Benj was trying to do when he found him. He even offered her a carrot, her favorite, but she just leaned her head down, unmoving.

"How is she?"

"I don't know what's wrong with her." Benj shook his head. "She seems lifeless."

"Perhaps she fell ill from something she ate?"

"No, milord." Tom, the stable master, came forward. "I checked to make sure the feed hadn't gone bad. It's fine. None of the other horses are ill. It's this mare, specifically."

"It's the one Brewer wanted to buy from your father." Benj scratched his chin. "I told him when he came by you weren't interested in selling. She was to be a brood mare."

"She won't be anyone's brood mare if we can't get her up and moving, but I'll keep trying, milord."

Silas nodded. "Benj, can I have a word?"

Benj stood from his crouched position in the stall. "Of course."

Silas led the way back inside and shut them in his father's study. Well, his study now, since he'd not only inherited his father's title, but all of his lands and wealth. Not that it mattered to him. He'd give anything to have the cranky old man back.

"What is bothering you?" Benj poured himself a drink and handed one to Silas.

"What makes you think something is bothering me?"

Benj shot him a baleful glare. "I may not be your brother by blood, but we are still brothers. I know you."

He was in a touchy mood.

"I keep remembering what you said the night Celia died, about it being unnatural, and you reminded me of that day your father nearly beat us to death. Why would you think of that the night my wife died?"

Benj downed his drink in one go and poured himself another before coming to sit down. "My father told me about that room the day I turned sixteen. He made me swear to never tell another soul, not even you."

That did not bode well.

"That room holds items that are cursed or could be used to do great evil. My father protects them."

"He protects them?" Silas gasped.

Benj held up a hand. "Not to keep them safe, but to keep them out of the hands of those who would use them. To keep others safe from them."

Silas still didn't like it. He was a devout man. He may not have always shown it, but his religion was important to him. His faith was the single most important thing to him besides his children.

"He made me swear to keep the items in that room, and any items brought to me, safe upon his deathbed. I understood by then. I'd seen the effects of a cursed item."

"You saw?"

Benj nodded. "There is a group of men who go and hunt down the evil in this world. They fight for people who are under siege from evil. My father sent me out with them so I would understand. In this case, it was a child's doll. The spirit within the doll convinced the child to allow it to enter her body. She was possessed, Silas. I've never seen anything like it. The things the girl said and did...it was unimaginable. She spoke perfect Latin. And she spoke in a language none of us understood, not even the priest who attended her."

The horror reflected in the man's eyes said more than any words to get the point across. He knew Benj as well as Benj knew him. What he'd seen disturbed him greatly. That much, Silas was sure of.

"The men I was with, they were able to free the girl and trap the spirit back into the doll. The cursed thing was locked away with all the rest of the forbidden horrors. I'm charged with keeping them from others now that Father is gone."

"I'm not sure what to say, Benj. It sounds so much like witchcraft to me, and you know how I feel about that."

"What those men do, it's blessed by the Church, Silas. Do you think I would allow it to continue in my home if it were not?"

"The Church knows?"

Benj sighed. "I was as shocked as you are, but I spoke with the archbishop himself in London, I was so concerned. They need men like us to help them safeguard the people who are unaware of the darkness all around them, to free those enslaved by evil. I came away with a heavy heart, but it's a burden I must bear. One that overshadows everything else."

"Is that what you think happened to Celia? That she came into possession of one of these cursed items?" If that were so, then it had to still be in the house. What if Mathilda found it? He stood, ready to go tear his wife's things apart for fear of his daughter finding it.

"Nay, Silas. Sit. What I think happened to Celia and mayhap even your father has nothing to do with a cursed item. I think it is something far more dangerous than that."

"Benj, whatever it is, just tell me. I cannot protect my family if I am in the dark." Even as he said the words, he shied away from them. Part of him wanted to remain unaware of the true evil that walked the realm.

"I was made aware of a great evil that had awoken and can only walk among us every few hundred years. It is a Fallen Angel that can reside within a living person for a short time. This particular evil feeds off the broken souls of children. That is why I was so concerned. It's why I was determined to save your son. I feared the trauma to his soul by the pain and fear he must have been in would have resulted in his soul being consumed by this Fallen."

"Then that would mean he had to have been in our home..." Silas's breath froze within his chest. "Brewer."

"I have no definitive proof of that, but I believe so. I've spoken with the shipyard he uses, and his family has done business with them for years, so he told the truth that night. On the surface, he appears innocent, but there is something there that bothers me. Something I can't define."

"He is not allowed back on this property," Silas spat. "Serene will protest, but she will get over it. Her life, as well as those of the children, are more important."

"Agreed, but something is off, Silas. This Fallen inhabits the body of a person whose soul is evil. From all accounts, Brewer is a kind man. Never a bad word for anyone, and he's gone out of his way to make sure his servants are well taken care of. I can find no instance of him doing anything remotely evil. I can't explain it, but he was the only stranger there the night Celia left us."

"And her labor came so suddenly. Her

71

bleeding spiked within a matter of minutes to the point there was no hope to save her." Silas sat back, disturbed. "Could he have used witchcraft on her?"

"I don't see how. We were right there. She was wearing jewelry I recognized. You gave her that necklace for her birthday, and she was fond of wearing it. The first thing I did was look for any object that was strange or unusual, but I found nothing. I even had her necklace tested, but nothing."

"When did you do this?"

"A few days after she died. You were so drunk you took note of nothing, and I had to try to find the source of the evil that took her from us. I wasn't about to let it fall into Serene's or Mathilda's hands, or one of the servants, for that matter."

"And you found nothing?"

"No, which only strengthens my suspicions about Brewer. If he had the Fallen inside, then no object would have been needed. He would have done it himself."

"You said you thought Father's death

was caused by this Fallen as well?"

Benj nodded. "Aye, I do. He was in good health until a few months ago. I questioned Serene about when she met Brewer, and she was not exactly honest with us. She led us to believe it was recently, but in truth, she'd been meeting him in town for several months. Around the time your father began to fall ill."

"But why would a creature who feeds off children care about an old man?"

"Mathilda," Benj said simply. "Ripping her mother from her and then her grandfather would cause her such pain, it would bruise her soul to a point that the creature could easily feed. He could also cause her death and take her soul for an eternity where it would be tortured so he could feed from it."

"What is this creature's name?"

"Deleriel. He is not the only Fallen, but he is more feared than any, other than the Morning Star."

Deleriel. Silas rolled the name around in his head, memorizing it. He'd learn all he could to protect those he loved.

"How do we stop him?"

"You cannot, my brother. We must be vigilant and protect the children until his time has passed. I spoke with the hunters and the Church in great detail about this, and there is no known weapon or even spell that can destroy him."

If he was made, he could be unmade. Of that, Silas was certain. No living creature could defy the laws of life and death. But was he living? He was a Fallen Angel, and Silas had no idea what an Angel was defenseless against. Yet another thing to research.

"Can you put me in touch with these men? I must learn all I can to keep my children safe."

"Aye. I can have Lincoln and his son come by tomorrow. I'll send a servant to their home forthwith."

"Thank you for looking out for us when I was unable." He owed his friend—nay, his brother—a debt that could never be repaid.

"Always, my friend. I will always find you and your kin and protect them with my dying breath. I swear it."

Silas looked up, speared the strange

aqua eyes, and something shivered through him. Walked over his soul just a little. He didn't doubt his friend's words, but he had to wonder what it would cost him. The heaviness in his heart worried him.

But that was a problem for another day.

For now, they had to protect the children.

Chapter Eight

"This isn't fair!" Serene shouted and stomped her foot. Silas had just informed her Evan Brewer would not be allowed back on the property and she was forbidden from seeing him again.

"No, it's not fair, and I'm sorry, but I have to do what's right for this family."

"How is not allowing me to marry the man I love right for me?" Tears soaked her cheeks. "I love him, Silas."

"You only think you love him, Serene."

"Did you only *think* you loved Celia, brother?" Anger simmered in her words, and Silas flinched away from it. "How can you deny me the same love you had? The happiness Celia brought to you? How is that right for me or for Evan?"

"There are things you do not know, Serene, things about him…"

"What things? That he's kind and gentle? That he would rather stay home than attend court and deal with all the politics? That he lives a simple life rather than the extravagance we were brought up with? It doesn't make him less worthy. I would think you'd want my future husband to be all those things."

"Serene, I understand you are upset, but my word is final on this. Do not test me. If I find that you have disobeyed me, you will not like the consequences."

"Just because you lost the love of your life, it does not mean you get take mine from me so I'm just as miserable as you are!"

She turned and stormed out of the study, slamming the door behind her.

Stunned, Silas stared at the door. How could she have said something so cruel to him? Even angry, Serene had never been cruel. It had to be Brewer's influence on her. It cemented his decision. Cutting her off from Brewer had been the right choice.

Silas slumped down in his father's chair. His chair, he reminded himself. He had to start thinking of his father's things as his. Maybe he'd take the children and Serene back to London to the townhouse he'd bought himself. The one Celia had decorated with such care.

To the town where Evan Brewer did not go.

He didn't know what to do, honestly. He was floundering. Ever since Benj had told him about this Fallen Angel, he'd been all mixed up. Confused, angry…vengeful.

If it was the very last thing he did, he would find a way to destroy this creature who had taken his wife from him.

There was a knock, and he bid them enter. Benj came in followed by two men he did not recognize. These men must be the hunters Benj told him of yesterday.

"Silas, allow me to introduce Lincoln Cooper, Earl of Lincolnshire, and his son, Frederick. I'm not sure you've met them before."

"Aye, I have." Silas stood and came around the desk to shake the men's hands. "We've attended a few of the same functions in London."

"It is good to see you again, my lord." Lincoln gripped his hand. "Allow me to deliver my family's condolences over the heavy loss you've suffered these last few weeks."

"Thank you," Silas murmured. "Please have a seat. Can I get you a drink?"

"That would be most welcome, given what we are about to discuss."

Silas poured them all a healthy drink, including the boy who looked to be about fourteen or so. He'd never met Lincoln's son, but he resembled his father. He was quiet, watchful. Silas hoped his own son was as studious in his efforts to pay attention to his surroundings and what was about to transpire.

"We examined your wife after...well, afterward, and we agree with Benjamin's assessment of the situation. We believe she came into contact with something that caused her death. We are not in agreement as to what that was, however."

"How can you be sure?" Silas asked, taking a seat next to his friend on the small sofa in the study.

"Whenever something particularly evil becomes activated, there's a residue left behind. There were black stains on your wife's abdomen. The stench of sulphur marked her body."

"Sulphur?"

"Sulphur is typically found when a demon is around. The scent alerts us more than anything else evil is afoot. The stain on her abdomen was a sticky substance we have found means a demon touched her. Now, that could be the demon itself, or it could be a cursed object. That is where our disagreement comes into play. Benjamin believes the demon was here, and we think it was an item."

"Demon?" Silas looked to Benj. "I thought you said it was a Fallen Angel."

"Fallen Angels are the first demons, my lord," Lincoln's son spoke up, his voice firm and sure. "It is from them lesser demons spring."

"This is all just so…"

"Hard to believe?" Lincoln asked.

"No. I was there. I saw what happened to Celia. It wasn't natural. It is overwhelming, that is all. I am trying to catch up so I can protect my children."

"Benjamin said he told you of the Fallen Angel we suspect?"

Silas nodded to Lincoln. "Yes. He fears my children are at risk. That is why you are here today, gentlemen. I will not allow any harm to come to them."

"We understand, my lord. Deleriel is particularly evil in that he tortures children. Our goal is the same as yours, to keep your children safe."

"And what can I do to ensure that?"

"While Fallen Angels are indestructible, we are not without recourse." Lincoln set his glass down on the small table between his and his son's chairs. "Over the centuries, our organization has found certain ancient runes and spells that can protect against Fallen Angels."

"Spells?" Silas tried not to overreact. It was all so much like witchcraft to him. It was abhorrent to do anything that might be seen as a crime against his religion.

Lincoln smiled, but it wasn't friendly. It was more sad than anything. "What we do is sanctioned by the Church, my lord. They know of each spell and each rune that is used to guard against evil. You will find the same ones within the walls of our own religion throughout Europe. Even the smaller parishes like we have here in the country. You are committing no sin, my lord."

Then why did he feel like he was?

"With your permission, we will ensure the safety of your home, especially the rooms where your children sleep."

"And the servants? What am I to tell them of what we are doing?"

"Tell them nothing. Give them leave to visit their families, and we will do this work while they are not in the house."

"My own home is secured in the same fashion," Benj said. "You and I can take the children and their nurse for a visit tomorrow. It would do good to get Serene out of the house as well. I'm assuming her anger is because you informed her of your decision regarding Brewer?"

Silas ran a hand through his hair. It was getting to be a little longer than he liked, but Celia had always admired his hair, so he let it grow out to the length she preferred. Perhaps he should cut it.

"Serene is not taking it at all well. She was cruel about it, using Celia's name to hurt me."

"Do not take it to heart, Silas. She is in pain too."

"Celia was like a sister to her. She's lost Celia, Father, and now the man she thinks she loves. I can understand that pain better than most. You are right, I know. It was just very painful to hear."

"Maybe it would do you some good to get away as well. You, Serene, and the children will come stay with me for a few weeks. They will be safe there, and not being in this house will help all of you begin to heal and deal with your grief."

"It would give you an excuse to get the servants out of the house," Lincoln agreed. "And if I may say so, my lord, I think Benjamin is right. This house is full of grief. Getting away from it will be good for you and your children."

"Fine. We shall travel to your country house tomorrow and have the servants sent home for the next two weeks. Will that give you time to do what you need to?"

"It will."

"I need to educate myself on this, gentlemen. Where do I start?"

"I have books and papers at my home you can read." Benj gripped his shoulder. "It's going to be fine, Silas. We will get through this."

Silas was not so sure about that, but he was going to do everything in his power to protect his family.

Chapter Nine

"I have a surprise for you, Mathilda."

Silas glanced up from where he sat playing with his daughter outside. They'd been at Benjamin's for a few days, and he decided to take a break from reading through all the journals and books and papers on the supernatural to play with his daughter. She demanded they go outside. Not that he blamed her. The child's nurse had been keeping her on a tight leash. Mathilda tended to break things. Since they were guests in Benj's home, he didn't disagree with the nurse about keeping his child in constant view.

But even the troublemaker that she

was, she needed to be let loose every once in a while.

"What is it, Uncle Benjy?" Her hazel eyes brightened with excitement, and she bounded up from where she sat making mud pies.

Benj's arm was hidden behind his back, and he pulled it out to reveal a tiny orange kitten. Mathilda squealed with delight and reached for it. The poor kitten clawed Benj's hands trying to get away from his new owner. Silas laughed while his friend winced.

"Easy, now, Mathilda. We must be easy with the kitten. He's still a baby, and we have to be careful of him."

"Like baby Ben?"

"Just like baby Ben." Benj went to his knees and showed the girl how to hold the kitten so it wouldn't scratch her. "I thought when you were missing your mother or your grandfather, this little guy would help."

"Thank you, Uncle Benjy!" She threw one arm around Benj and noisily kissed his cheek. Silas was grateful for his friend in that moment, for being able to make his daughter smile when she was in such pain.

"What are you going to name him?" Silas asked.

"Rupert," she answered promptly, and both he and Benj burst into laughter. That girl certainly was fixated on the name Rupert.

"Well, better your kitten than your brother." Benj ruffled the girl's hair. "Take your kitten to the kitchens and get him some milk. I rescued him from the barn, so I'm sure he's hungry."

Mathilda wasted no time in running toward the manor house screeching about milk.

"You've ruined any chance I have of finding her a birthday present even half as good as that one."

Benj dropped down beside him. "That was the point. Uncles trump fathers."

Silas snorted. "You were right about us coming here. She seems less unhappy."

"There are no reminders of her mother here." Benj turned his attention to Silas. "And you? Has being here helped you?"

Silas nodded. "Aye. Not looking at her

things lying about helped more than anything, but I can't bring myself to tell the servants to pack them away."

"That's not something you need to do right away. When you're ready, you'll be ready."

Silas had no idea how to thank Benjamin for all he'd done for him and his family. He'd seen to the protection of the children when Silas couldn't. He had no words strong enough to express his gratitude.

"I wondered when you were going to leave my private library."

"Mathilda needed to be let loose before she began to play pirates around your breakables."

"That girl. She should have been a boy."

"God help us when she gets old enough to marry. I'm not sure there's a gent alive who can keep up with her now, let alone when she's sixteen."

Benj laughed. "Think we'll survive the next eleven years until we can marry her off?"

"I sincerely hope so. She scares her

nurse on a daily basis. I heard her muttering once that the girl was the child of Satan."

"Speaking of, how are your studies coming along? Learning what you wanted to?"

Silas had come to the realization early on that he'd never learn enough. The things he had discovered were real were the things of nightmares, and still, he found even more to be terrified of. An entire world existed alongside their own, and most went about their business unaware. He'd be better off now knowing about that secret world, but at the same time, he was now more equipped to protect himself and his family.

"I feel as if I've only scratched the surface. Part of me wishes I never discovered what lives in the darkness."

"I am the same. I had nightmares for weeks after that initial encounter, but I know the burden of knowledge we carry is necessary for keeping the balance of good and evil. It's men like you and me and Lincoln and his son who hold the line in the dark."

"You sound like a poet."

"The ladies enjoy my monologue."

He shoved his friend good-naturally and then turned serious. "Now that I know about this, I feel I must help in any way I can. Whether it is gold or my sword arm that is needed."

"I knew you would. There is plenty of time for that. First, you must acquaint yourself with the knowledge needed to survive in this world, and then we will see about getting you more involved."

"Have you seen Serene?" Silas changed the subject. Until he'd gotten through more material, he'd hold his questions.

"She's locked herself in her room. I sent one of the maids up to check on her, as she's even locked her handmaiden out. I thought maybe someone new would help her mood, but alas, she refused the woman entry."

"I wish I could help her, but unless I tell her of these unspeakable things, I do not know how to ease her pain."

"It is best she not know of our suspicions, or even of the world you are now admitted into. It would only cause her more worry."

"I know, but seeing her in pain is almost more than I can bear. She hates me, Benj."

"Nay, brother, she does not. She's spitting mad and taking it out on everyone, but the girl is incapable of true hate. Her gentle heart would not know how to process such a thing."

If Benj had heard how she had spoken to Silas that day in the study, he might not be so quick to defend. "I think Brewer influenced her. She seems more distant, more withdrawn. Her anger is a living thing."

"Then it is good she is here. Brewer came by the house this morning. He was denied entry, and I emphasized your decision regarding his marriage proposal."

"How did he take it?"

"He seemed more sad than angry. I swear, I think I am wrong about him at times. It was as if I pulled his heart from his chest and crushed it in front of him this morning. But he is the only unknown in this situation."

"Lincoln said he disagreed about a cursed object being involved. What did he mean?"

"For Deleriel to have been there himself, he believes I would have sensed it. I've become more accustomed to evil and how to fight it. But that night, I felt nothing. He thinks it was because there was a cursed item involved, but I checked everything, down to the silverware on the table. I promise you, there was nothing."

"Could Brewer have moved it when we raced upstairs?"

Benj sighed heavily. "Maybe."

"But you don't think so."

"As I said, I am fairly certain I would have sensed something, had that been the case, just as I should have sensed it if a Fallen was among us. I feel like I let you down, Silas. I, of all people, should have been able to prevent what happened to Celia."

"Nay, Benj, do not blame yourself. It was not your fault."

His friend's shoulders slumped. "But it feels like it is."

"I feel guilty too. Had she not been pregnant, she would never have died, and that is entirely my fault."

"Do not say such things." Benj glared at him. "Do you regret your son? The child his mother gave her life to bring into this world?"

"You misunderstand. I do not regret my son. I did blame him for a while, I am ashamed to admit, but that is gone now. My only thoughts are to keep him safe."

"We'll both keep him and his sister safe. Now, what say we go rescue the kitchen staff from your daughter and Rupert?"

Silas stood and followed Benj into the house, his thoughts troubled. He only hoped he could keep his promise of keeping his children safe.

Chapter Ten

"I see you have decided to grace us with your presence," Silas said as his sister sat down at the dining table. She looked pale, and he worried about how hard all this had been on her, but if he showed even a moment's weakness, she would pounce on it. She was very much like Mathilda that way.

"I am sorry for the way I behaved these last few days." She looked him directly in the eye. "I am unsure of what came over me or where that anger came from. It is not me. I deeply regret the words I said to you, brother. Can you forgive me?"

"It is already forgiven." Now, this was

the Serene he knew and loved. Getting her away from Brewer had been the right decision. "Have you visited your niece today?"

"No, why? Is something wrong?" Real alarm colored her expression. He should have been more careful in his choice of words after everything she had lost.

"No, nothing is wrong. Benj has given her a kitten. I thought she would have shown you her new prize."

"A kitten?" A soft smile played with her lips. "What did she name it?"

"Rupert." Benj nodded to the servants to begin serving.

"Rupert?" Serene all but choked on the name. "Wherever did she come up with that name?"

"She told me one of the fairies that lives in the rose garden is named Rupert. She liked the name."

"Fairies?" Serene laughed. "To be five again and believe in magic."

"Would that we could all be that innocent again," Benj said and picked up his spoon. "Are you feeling better, my beauty?"

"I am. I still do not understand why you have denied Evan his request, but you are my brother, Silas, and only want what is best for me. You would never do something to hurt me if you could spare me."

"I would not. Know that I have my reasons, reasons you do not need to understand, but it is to protect you."

Serene nodded, bowing her head. "Then I will accept your decision."

"It appears a change of scenery has done you well, my beauty." Benj pointed his spoon at Serene. "Tell me, do you still think you are in love with Brewer?"

"I…" Serene cleared her throat. "I do not know, Benjamin. It is strange, like a fog surrounds my memories. I think of him, and I get this pressure on my chest, and I wonder if it is because I miss him, but…"

"But you do not need to worry about it anymore," Benj told her. "Silas and I will find you a husband who will treat you with the care and devotion you deserve. One who will take you to all the balls and make sure you're the envy of every other woman in attendance."

"And you, Benjamin, when are you going to wed?"

"Not for years and years." He winked. "I still enjoy my wild ways too much."

"Many men would continue those wild ways even if wed," she countered.

"Not I." He put his spoon down and looked directly at her. "When I marry, I would never disrespect my wife by continuing with affairs and mistresses."

"That is very gallant of you."

"No, my beauty. It is simply the truth."

Silas knew as well as Benjamin what she was asking. Serene had had her eye set on his friend since she was Mathilda's age. Only Benj looked at her like his little sister and not a potential wife. He would never marry her. Silas hoped Serene gave up on that notion, but he suspected now that Brewer was out of the picture, she would truly begin her campaign to win over Benj.

God help them all.

The rest of dinner was filled with light conversation, if not laughter. It was more than they'd had in weeks. Serene was more like her old self with perhaps a glint of a challenge. Poor Benj.

Silas bid his sister goodnight and took a walk in the gardens. He and Benj had spent many a day here running amongst the roses and playing pirate when they were boys. It was here he'd seen Celia for the first time. His father had dragged him to the ball Benj's parents had hosted. A Christmas ball. She'd escaped to the gardens to get away from all the young men vying for her attention.

She had been beautiful with her blonde hair swept up on her head and a silvery blue gown that caught the moonlight and seemed to shimmer. He had been entranced and promptly introduced himself. She had sighed and turned to go back inside, but he snatched her hand and asked her if she had ever seen the roses at night.

Celia loved roses. It was the first thing he'd learned about her. Benj's mother had forced the two of them to help her plant a lot of the flowers, and so Silas knew enough to be able to name them off to her. He had thought he'd impressed her, but apparently, he had not. When he called on her the very next day, she'd refused to see him.

Thankfully, her father had not been so adamant and had seen him. Silas stated his intentions, and their fathers had done the rest.

He would never forget that first moment, though. She had ensnared him like no other, and he feared no other woman would come close to the feelings she'd brought out in him. He did know one thing. He would never remarry. He would raise his children and be grateful for the time he did have with the love of his life.

He hoped one day both his sister and his best friend found the same kind of love. Whoever they ended up with, he prayed it would be the love of a lifetime.

And that they had more years with their loves than he had his.

Silas took one last look around and dragged himself back into Benj's library. He had more reading to do before he could find the lonely solitude of his bed.

Chapter Eleven

A week passed, and chaos ensued. Between the baby crying all hours of the day and night and Mathilda running through the house carrying a squalling kitten, Silas thought Benj was sure to be glad to be rid of them when they left.

Silas closed the book he'd been reading and sat back. The house was quieter than he'd heard it in days, and he wondered where his daughter was. Hopefully, not hatching any sort of plan that involved damaging property. Her nurse stayed on top of things, though, and would find him if she were into too much trouble.

There was a knock at the library door, and it opened to reveal Lincoln and Benj. They strode into the room, closing the door behind them.

"Your home has been demon-proofed, my lord. Even against the Fallen. You should be safe to take your family home."

"Will the servants notice anything unusual?"

"No, my lord. All the necessary runes are well hidden within the house. The servants will not see them."

"Very good. You have my thanks."

"I wish we had been able to prevent what happened, but at least we can…" He broke off, and both he and Benj stiffened.

"What is it?"

"I am not sure…" Benj cocked his head. "Something feels off."

"What do you mean?"

Instead of answering, he opened the door and called for his butler. The man came within a moment.

"Henderson, do we have any visitors, aside from my guest?"

"No, milord. Were you expecting someone?"

Benj shook his head. "No, I thought I heard someone, that's all. Thank you, Henderson."

"Of course, milord." The man took his leave, but Benj did not return. Instead, he walked farther out into the hallway and stood there, listening.

"The protection spell is broken."

"How can you tell?" Silas asked. He felt nothing unusual.

"My blood was used to create it. I felt it snap just now."

"We must get to the children!" Lincoln declared. "Where are they?"

"Probably upstairs. The baby has been fussy, and I doubt Molly would allow Mathilda out of her sight even if she's tending to the babe."

The three of them ran up the stairs and crashed through the door of the room that had been given to Mathilda. She was on the floor playing with her kitten. Molly, their nurse, looked up from where she sat reading, the baby asleep on her lap.

"My lords? Is something wrong?"

"No, no." Silas let out a breath he didn't realize he was holding. "Well, yes.

We believe there is an intruder on the grounds. Lock the door and open it for no one but us. Can you do that?"

"Of course, my lord."

"Papa?" Mathilda looked up with wide eyes.

"Nothing to worry about, my darling girl. Papa will keep you safe."

She winced when her kitten sank his claws into her hand. "Ouch, Rupert. Bad kitty."

"You stay in this room until Papa comes to get you, Mathilda. And listen to Molly. No nonsense from you."

"Yes, Papa."

"Do you promise?"

She nodded.

"Papa needs you to say the words."

"I promise."

"Good girl." He looked to Molly. "Lock this door behind us."

He waited until he heard the lock click before going to Serene's bedchamber. She wasn't there, though, and panic struck him.

"Do you think Brewer is here? Could she be with him?"

"Let us not jump to conclusions. She could be in the kitchens, the sitting room, or the gardens. We'll find her."

"I can't lose her too, Benj, not after Father and Celia. I just can't."

"You're not going to. We'll find her."

They checked every room upstairs, and Benj even checked the locked door leading to the attic space where all the items he protected were kept. It was still locked tight.

Downstairs proved just as futile. Serene was nowhere to be found. Lincoln checked the garden while he and Benj raced to the stables. His sister loved to ride, and the weather was perfect for riding.

She was leaning into the stall of her favorite horse, a white mare that had the gentlest disposition Silas had ever seen. He'd even tried to purchase the animal from Benj, but he had refused to sell.

Serene glanced up, startled, when they came running into the barn. "Silas? Benjamin?"

"Thank God," Silas whispered as he hugged her to him. "I thought…"

"What?" she asked, her voice muffled from where he held her so tightly. "What is wrong?"

"We have an intruder on the property," Benj said. "We couldn't find you."

"An intruder?" She pulled away from Silas. "How do you know?"

"That is of no concern. Until we have the intruder in custody, you need to go to your room and lock the door."

"The children?"

"Locked safely in Mathilda's room with Molly."

"Of course. Whatever you say. Is it safe to go alone? There's a good bit of distance between here and the house."

"We will escort you." Benj took her arm and all but dragged her out of the barn. Silas wondered if his friend's feelings for Serene went a little deeper than he thought. He'd been just as panicked, and the grip he had on Serene was quite possessive. He tucked that away for later. Right now, they needed to ascertain if Brewer was on the property and if he had a Fallen with him.

Once Serene was safely locked within

her bedchamber, Silas and Benj met back up with Lincoln. The servants were informed there might be an intruder on the grounds and were told to fan out and search the property.

Benj and Lincoln set about systematically searching every single sigil that was etched into the property to secure the protection circle around it. Given Benj's family estate was just as massive as Silas's, it took a while.

They were about a mile from the main house when they found it. The sigil had been engraved into a tree. You would have to physically climb the tree to even get to it, but a slash had been carved through the middle of the design, effectively nullifying it.

Benj was able to restore the design, but it took another hour, and by the time they arrived back at the house, it was well past dark. The three men wearily went inside, looking for a drink and a hot meal.

They called out for Henderson and asked for just that when he appeared. "Has all been well here while we were searching the property?"

"Yes, milord. No one came to the house, and dinner was delivered to the children and your sister a while ago."

The three men sat down at the dining room table and had a cold dinner of salted chicken and roasted vegetables. They told the staff not to bother to heat it up for them. They were too hungry to wait.

"We found no evidence of Brewer, but someone disabled that sigil." Lincoln bit into his chicken. "What do you suppose his purpose was?"

"Serene," Benj said, his voice cold. "He will not get her. He or Deleriel."

"Deleriel would have no use for her," Lincoln said.

"Perhaps that was Brewer's price for allowing Deleriel to use him as a host. He wanted Serene, and Deleriel could deliver the girl to him."

Silas had not looked at it like that. His blood ran cold thinking of what might have happened to his sister had they not found her before she went riding.

"I would feel better had we found Brewer," Benj continued. "I don't like that the protection wards came down and we found nothing."

"Be grateful no harm came from today." Lincoln wiped his mouth. "It could have been so much worse."

Silas agreed. The threat to his children was great, but he did not discount the threat to his sister. If everything he'd learned about Deleriel were true, then the Fallen's host had to be truly evil down to their soul. His sister had escaped a fate that might be worse than death.

The men finished their meal in silence, and once they'd said goodbye to Lincoln, they climbed the stairs to check on Serene and the children.

"Benj, can I ask you something?"

"Of course."

"Are you sure you don't have feelings for Serene?"

"I love her like she's my own sister."

Silas debated if he should say anything further, but decided he had to. "It is just that at the barn, the way you took hold of her it is the way I would have taken hold of Celia, not my sister."

Benj stopped outside Mathilda's room

and frowned, clearly startled. "I was scared, that is the honest truth, but—"

The baby's cry interrupted him. "I think we should have the physician come and give him a once-over. He's been crying for days on end with no sign of stopping."

"Mayhap you are right." Silas tried the knob, but it was locked. Of course. He had told Molly to keep it locked. "Molly, open the door."

There was no response from the maid, and he knocked on the door. "Molly?"

Benj frowned when again there was no response. Something wasn't right, and Silas put his shoulder to the heavy door, forcing the lock to give, and it burst inward, carrying him with it.

The sight that greeted him chilled his blood.

Serene stood in front of the fireplace, Ben in her arms. She was covered in blood and held a wicked looking blade in one hand. His eyes took in the sight without really seeing because he was focused on the small heap in the middle of the floor.

Blonde curls stained with blood fanned out around her head, her kitten huddled against a chest that was unmoving.

No.

He dropped to his knees, his mind frozen, unable to look away from his darling girl lying dead on the floor. Molly was in a similar heap a few feet away.

"Serene, put the baby down."

Benj's words cut through his numbness.

She had his son.

"No. A price was asked and must be paid."

"Price?" Benj came farther into the room.

"You are both fools. You thought poor Evan was somehow involved, but he wasn't. He was my way out. If you had just allowed the marriage, none of this would have been necessary. He is easy to control, and I would have been free to do as I pleased."

"Did you make a deal, Serene?" Benj crept closer to her, but her gaze was fixated on the baby in her arms. He was crying.

"Yes. Once you cut off my escape route, I had to. Deleriel knew you would. He warned me of it, but I did not believe him. Evan was such a kind, honest man, and I did not think you'd find fault with him."

"The night Celia died, he was there, wasn't he?"

She nodded. "He was with me and not Evan as you both suspected."

"But you are not evil, sister." Silas couldn't grasp what she was saying.

She smiled. "It is easy to fool those who do not wish to see."

Silas thought back to that day he'd found her reading a book of sorcery. He'd thought it was harmless, and he'd gotten rid of it, but what if it wasn't? What if she'd been reading books like that for who knew how long? He had traveled a lot for business once his father grew ill. He couldn't be certain.

All he'd ever seen when he looked at her was his baby sister.

"How could you do this to Mathilda? She loved you."

"And I loved her as best I could. It's

why her and Ben's souls were not part of the deal I made. Deleriel will not gain that much."

"Then why do this?" Silas raged, standing. His anger snapped him out of his daze, and he turned from the lifeless body of his child and toward the one person he trusted more than anyone. She was his flesh and blood, and his daughter adored her.

"Because I had to sacrifice that which I loved the most, and that would be the children. I want out of this life, out of a forced marriage and to be able to do as I please. Deleriel can give that to me, and I'm taking it."

Benj tackled her, knocking the knife from her hand and grabbing for the baby.

Serene howled and kicked, landing a solid blow to the man's most sensitive area. Benj merely grunted and wrenched the baby from her. Silas took him the second he was free, leaving Benj to subdue his sister.

His body shook with grief as he collapsed onto the floor next to his beautiful daughter. Even in death, she was his darling girl. A single tear ran its course down his face, falling onto her cheek. He pulled her to him, his little girl in one arm and his son in the other.

How had this happened?

How had he not seen?

The danger, the threat had been under his own roof all this time.

"And Celia? Was that you?"

"That was Deleriel. I had no control over what happened when he was active."

"He wanted the children."

"Yes, but I made sure he'd never get their souls, Silas. As cold as I am, they matter to me."

"But not enough. You killed her."

"The world is about sacrifice, brother. We must be willing to sacrifice to gain the things that matter."

"Your freedom meant more than your niece's life? More than Celia's life? More than Ben's life?"

"Yes."

Benj's arms tightened around her, and she snarled.

Silas stood, his children in his arms. "If you were willing to take their lives, then you'll be willing to pay for their lives with your own."

"Silas, no." Benj's words stopped him. "Killing her solves nothing."

"It solves everything!"

"It doesn't. She made a deal. In death, she'll still get what she wants."

"That's right, she will."

Benj's arms fell away, and he stumbled back from Serene, whose eyes had turned black. It was not her voice that spoke either, but that of a man.

Deleriel.

Silas snarled, and Benj held him back. "No. You cannot hurt him, and he would destroy you. Think of your son."

"What did you do to my sister?"

"I did nothing to her. I only asked if I could join her for a short while. I promised her a way out and arranged it, but you took that from her. If you want someone to blame for your child's death, blame yourself."

Silas's knees nearly buckled with that truth—and it *was* truth. If he had not forbidden the marriage, then she would never have made a deal. Mathilda would still be alive.

"Now, gentlemen, we must go. Your sister has only fulfilled part of her bargain with me, and for that, she will pay a price. Of that, I assure you."

And before their eyes, Serene disappeared. She was standing there one minute and gone the next.

Leaving Silas alone with the most heart-wrenching grief he'd ever known in his life.

Chapter Twelve

Benj,

Do you remember when we were boys playing in our mothers' gardens? We would pretend all sorts of things, and in the end, we always prevailed against whatever we fought. Things were so simple then, and I wish for those days again. I wish the things we know of now didn't exist, or at least that we did not know they did.

It would have been kinder.

I have thought long and hard upon this path I have set myself. But too much has been taken from me. I should have seen, but who would suspect one's own flesh and blood housed an evil so great, it defied logic? Celia, my father, and Mathilda, their deaths are on my hands. And I have to make that right.

I have taken these past few weeks to get my affairs in order. Everything has been turned over to you. I have entrusted my son into your care as well. Raise him to be the man I know you are, to be a man we can both be proud of. Tell him his father loved him and will one day avenge his sister and his mother.

You told me once that Deleriel could not be killed. But I do not believe that. What was made can be unmade, and if it takes me an eternity to do it, I will. That, I promise.

And then there is poppet. She will pay for what she did to Mathilda. For betraying the trust of such an innocent who did nothing wrong but love her.

I must do these things, and to accomplish this, I must do things that go against everything I believe in and who I am. But I will do them because it is the only way to avenge my family.

You are my brother in my heart, and I

am entrusting you with my son, the most precious thing left to me in this life. I know you will do right by him. Raise him as you do your own son. Give him the father he deserves. Teach him to laugh, to fight, to love. Teach him all the things I will not be able to.

Raise Ben to know about the dangers in the dark so he can guard against them. Teach him to keep others safe. Make him a warrior against evil. Tell him what happened to his mother and to his sister, and even his grandfather. Do not let him be blind in this world.

And above all else, love him as I do. As I always will, no matter what I become. I will always love him. Make sure he knows that.

Be well, my friend, my brother.
Regards,
Silas Haversham, Duke of Kent

Chapter Thirteen

Benjamin,
You are named after my father and the man who will become your father. It is a good, strong name and one I know you will live up to. You came into this world brutally, and for that, I am sorry. You were ripped away from your mother before you ever had the chance to know her. She told me from the beginning you were a boy. She was so proud to be carrying the next Duke of Kent.

But more than that, she loved you. I would catch her sometimes rubbing her swollen belly and talking to you. She would tell you tales of pirates, the same ones I told you sister, Mathilda. Like your mother, you will never know her, but she loved you as well. She wanted to name you Rupert, but Benj and I saved you from that fate, at least.

Celia saw the best in everyone, and I hope that carries over to you. She could always sympathize with even the worst of people. I envied her that. I tried, but I hardly ever succeeded. The one place I never thought I would have to try is with my own family. It is something I will regret for the rest of my days. Had I seen what was right in front of me, your mother and your sister might still be with us.

I don't know if you will ever understand why I left, why I need to find a way to avenge your mother and your sister. Never think it is because you are not enough for me. You are. I love you, my son, with my entire heart and soul. I will love you for all my days. You give me the strength I need to go out and avenge those who were taken from us through evil.

You and I have lost so much, but I must

take your father from you now. I do it not by choice, but by necessity. I have charged Benj to tell you what transpired the nights your mother and your sister died. I cannot bring myself to write it down here. It is too painful, and I feel so much guilt because I did not see the viper within our midst.

I was not able to protect your mother or your sister, and it is a shame that will haunt me for an eternity.

But I will make it right.

And that is why I must leave, why I must do unspeakable things to make those responsible pay for what they have stolen from us.

I hope you can forgive me for leaving you, but I cannot live in a world where I allowed what happened to our family to remain unavenged, where I did not do everything within my power to set right what Deleriel and Serene did.

Grow into a strong man who takes up the cause of the innocent and the victims. Fight against the growing dark because it is only through men like you and Benj that humanity stands a chance at survival. Be well, my son, and I know I love you.

Your father,
Silas Haversham, Duke of Kent

Chapter Fourteen

Silas stroked the downy skin of his son's cheek one last time and turned, going out of the room and closing the door behind him. He made his way downstairs to Benj's private library. He left the letters on the man's desk then walked out of the house, leaving his life as Silas Haversham behind him forever.

It took him three days to reach the crossroads. It had to be a specific one, and thanks to all the reading he had done these last few weeks, he knew exactly where to find it.

He took out the small box containing the things required and buried the box.

Then he sat down to wait. He was specific, identifying Deleriel by name in the summoning.

His time on this Earth had passed, but Silas was not worried. The Fallen would find a way. He had been summoned, after all.

Silas sat there in the dirt for hours before he felt the shift in the air. The smell of sulphur invaded his nostrils, and he stood. The wind picked up, and he waited. There was no fear in him.

He had nothing left to fear.

His only goal was vengeance, and he would do what he must. God may not forgive him for what he was about to do, but it mattered not. Nothing mattered anymore, save one thing.

The old man who appeared was hunched in on himself, his clothes ragged and his eyes covered in a white film. His steel gray hair was matted, and his hands gnarled.

"You summoned me?"

Deleriel. It was the same voice that had come out of Serene's mouth that night. It was a voice he would never forget.

"I want to make a deal, demon."

"What do you want, Silas Haversham, Duke of Kent?"

"My sister."

He laughed. "You want to save your sister's soul?"

"No."

"No?" Deleriel cocked his head.

"Her soul was gone a long time ago. I do not want to save her. I want to kill her for what she did. I want to make her suffer for stealing my daughter's life. I want her to hurt, to scream in agony and suffering. I want her to beg for mercy. Mercy I will not give her."

"You sound like one of mine."

"A man can only take so much before he breaks. I broke. And now, all that is left to me is vengeance."

"And you think I will help you? Serene is one of mine now. She is living the life she wants until her contract comes due, and then her soul resides with me for eternity."

"Then what must I do to buy that contract from you? To buy her soul from you?"

"In my world, souls are power, the only form of currency that matters, and one soul is greater than all the wealth of the known world combined. It is not something that is easily bought."

"Name your price, demon."

"Five hundred thousand souls, not including yours."

"Done. On one condition. I keep mine."

"Why would you want to keep it? By the time you are done collecting souls, yours will be so black, it will be worthless."

"But it will still be mine. I will get you your five hundred thousand souls for Serene's. No matter how long it takes, I will do it."

"Then you have a deal, Silas David Haversham, Duke of Kent. Five hundred thousand souls for your sister's, and you shall keep your own."

He held out his hand, and Silas took it. The gnarled joints of the old man's hands had straightened, but the fingernails dug into Silas's skin, drawing blood.

The deal was done, cemented in blood.

He turned his eyes to the moon, and he felt the darkness creep into him, flowing from Deleriel. His sense of right and wrong blurred, his values and morality disappearing until there was nothing left but the darkness and the need to hurt, to take. Nothing but evil.

Except that one bright spark of light that remained. His soul. He had kept it so as not to lose the pain of his family's deaths. Pain would drive him to do what must be done to avenge his family.

And from this day forth, he would work toward not only getting his hands on his sister but finding a way to defeat Deleriel.

As God and Hell were his witness, they would be avenged.

Chapter Fifteen

The table was quiet as Silas finished his story.

"I am so sorry, Uncle Silas." Benny got up from where he sat and hugged Silas for all he was worth.

The boy's arms tightened, and Silas hugged him back. That story had eaten away at him for centuries. He felt no better sharing it, but he felt no worse. He was just numb.

"I understand, Silas." Mattie deserted her chair and came to stand by him. "What she did, it had nothing to do with Deleriel, but it wasn't your fault."

"It *was* my fault." No one would ever

change his mind.

"Either way, you did what you set out to do. Deleriel is dead, and your sister..." She broke off and took a deep breath. "The reaper in me wants to save her, but I won't. She deserves to suffer."

Silas looked up, shocked.

Mattie smiled. "I'm not the same person I was, but in a way, I am still very much the same. Dan only sees the good in me, and I try to only listen to the good in me, but I am who I am. I am Mattie Louise Hathaway, foster kid and survivor. I blur the lines all the time. I understand hitting first and asking for forgiveness later. I do what has to be done, no matter the cost to me or those around me. I've stolen things, I've hurt people, and I've been hurt. I've been broken, and I wouldn't change anything about all of that. It made me who I am. Just as it did you."

He gripped her hand. "I'm a demon. I traded my humanity to avenge my family. I studied everything I could find on the Fallen and on Angels in general. I made deals to gain what I needed. I killed innocents in my pursuit to destroy Deleriel, and I almost got you killed."

"You did what you had to do, Silas. I would have done the same. You and I are more alike than anyone else. We understand each other, and we understand sacrifice and self-hatred and blame. I meant what I said to you a few weeks ago. I forgive you, Silas, so I think it's time you forgave yourself."

"I don't know if I can."

"You family would have wanted you to."

"I am not sure of that. Given what I have become and the things I did, I do not think Celia would have been proud to call me husband."

"She might not, but I'm proud to call you my grandfather. You and I will never see eye to eye on things, and I am a little terrified of you, but you're my family, all the same. For a foster kid, that matters. So take what I say to heart. Your past is your past. Stay in the here and now with me."

"I'm not so sure young Daniel would appreciate that."

"He'll get over it."

"I almost killed him too."

"But you protected him. You hid him from a reaper, and you've given him the same protections you gave me. It might take him a while, but he'll come around."

"He will," Benny promised. "My brother is smart like that."

"Indeed, he is," Silas said and gently moved the boy from around his neck. "How would you like some chocolate cake?"

"With the blueberry syrup?"

Silas laughed at the boy's eagerness. "My friend Benj loved chocolate cake too."

"He had eyes like mine."

"He did."

"Is he related to me?" Benny asked.

All things come full circle. That was what his father always said. Silas walked away from his child and his best friend. He sat here now with his granddaughter and a child who came from his best friend's lineage. He was full circle.

"Yes, Benny, he was."

"Then I'm glad you told me the story.

It means we're all family."

"Yes, Benny, we are. Now, let's go find the chocolate cake. I have a soul to collect later."

Family.

It was more than a demon could ask for.

Thus concludes the Ghost Files Series. Turn the page to get a sneak peek at Homecoming (The Crane Diaries #1) where Mattie's story is continued in New Orleans!

HOMECOMING

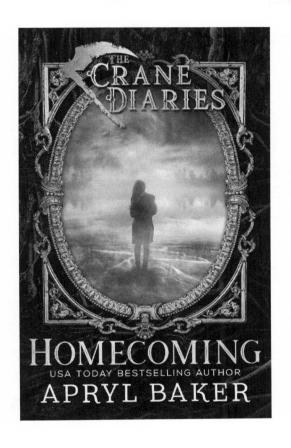

THE CRANE DIARIES 1

BY APRYL BAKER

"You're insane."

I've heard worse. But maybe he's right. Maybe I am insane. Why else would I be on the roof a house trying to talk a ghost down? He's already dead, so why am I trying to talk him out of jumping?

Because he needs to move on, that's why. And that *is* my job. I'm a living reaper. I convince ghosts they need to move on and stop haunting the living. It never works out well. I mean, if they stay here long enough, they'll go crazy and start hurting people. That's something we don't want.

Now, if only Kane will shut up and let me work, we'll all be fine.

The guy can't be more than eighteen or twenty. Red hair, his white face splattered with an abundance of freckles, and he's tall. Freakishly tall, basketball player tall, but really thin, giving his face more of a hawk-like look. The determined way he's staring at the ground below him makes me crawl along the shingles faster. If I don't reach him, I'll have to come back tomorrow and try again.

"Hey, you!" I shout, knowing I can't startle him into falling. "You there, about to jump off the roof."

At first, he doesn't even respond, but after a moment, he turns his head and looks at me. Blue eyes watch as I finally make the last few feet of the roofline to where he's standing.

"Why are you still up here jumping off the roof?" I stand, my legs a little shaky.

He looks from me to the ground below him, frowning. I think I confused him.

"I'm Emma." I inch closer. "I'm here to help you."

"Nobody can help me." His voice is flat, toneless, but it carries the scratchiness of the dead. It's a sound that always slithers along my spinal cord and makes me shiver.

"Yes, I can." I inch a little closer until I'm standing beside him, looking down at the ground. Jeez, it's high. One good wind, and I could easily fall. Or the ghost guy could get annoyed and push me. I'm not discounting either option.

"No." The guy shakes his head. "There is no help for me. I only have one option left."

"To jump. I know." I take a deep breath, steeling myself against the cold creeping into my bones. "You already did that. A long time ago."

The ghost shakes his head, anger starting to bleed into his fathomless blue eyes. "Go away."

"Sorry, can't. I need you to understand you're already dead so I don't have to come back tomorrow. I have plans."

"What are you talking about?"

"What's your name?"

"Steve." His frown deepens. "Why

won't you go away and leave me alone?"

"Because I'm a reaper, and my job is to make you understand you don't belong here anymore. You already died, and your ghost is stuck here, repeating your death over and over every day at this exact same time."

"You're crazy."

Sometimes it would be easier if I were crazy.

I turn around, my back to the ground, and ignore Kane's warning shout from below. He's supposed to be my trainer in all things reaping, but most days he's yelling at me not to take so many chances. Yada, yada, yada.

Closing my eyes, I focus on the most loving memories I have. I think about warmth and joy, and before I know it, the softest glow bathes my closed eyes. There it is. Sure enough, a glowing yellow haze has appeared before us, growing until it's an opening into the very air around us. The other side.

"See?" I toss the ghost a grin. "There's the light. You don't have to stay here, jumping and dying every day for an eternity. You can move on, find your family, be at peace."

"What is that?" he whispers, taking a step closer. All ghosts inherently want to move on, but sometimes they can't for whatever reason.

"The next life?" I make it a question, because honestly, I'm not really sure. I know he'll be ferried through the Between, the plane between this world and the afterlife, and then be judged. I don't tell him that little fact. I'm guessing he's still here because he feels guilty about killing himself.

"Who are you?" He takes another tiny step closer to the light.

"I'm Emma Rose Crane."

"I…Jason?" He squints, looking into the light. Most ghosts will see the reapers who come for them as someone important to them, usually a family member who has died. Parents, grandparents, siblings. Or sometimes childhood friends.

"Who's Jason?" I shuffle along with him. I can't force him to go into the light. He has to do it himself, but I can try to persuade him all I want.

"My cousin. He died when we were kids."

Bingo. "See, Jason's there waiting for you. He doesn't want you hurting anymore. There's no reason for you to keep jumping to your death."

"What are you talking about?" He turns to face me, confusion stamped all over his face. "I would never kill myself."

"But I've seen you jump from this roof every day for the last week at exactly the same time."

"No, I didn't. I wouldn't. We don't believe in that."

This doesn't make sense. I've seen him jump myself. "Then why are you up here on the roof, Steve?"

"I was thinking about stuff. It's where I come to be alone."

"Stuff?"

He sighs but inches closer to the light. "I want to tell my family about Mark, but I don't know how they'll react."

Ohhhh, he's afraid of telling them he's gay. Is it possible he fell by accident?

That he came up here to think and accidentally went off the roof? Makes sense, I guess.

"I promised Mark I'd tell them, but I don't know how. My dad...he's not going to take it well at all. He's hardcore religious."

"Steve." I lay a gentle hand on him. He's still full of energy, probably not long dead. If this was his house, his family must have moved. It's empty now. "You don't have to tell them anything anymore. You're dead."

"I'm not dead. I was just talking to my sister a few minutes ago."

"Look around." I sweep my hand at the empty landscape. "The house is empty, there are no cars here except for mine. No one lives here anymore. You died, and they moved on. Now it's your turn to move on. Jason's waiting for you. All you have to do is step into the light."

"I'm really dead?" He shuffles closer until he's almost touching the light. He's not looking at it, though. His eyes are sweeping the abandoned farmhouse's yard, listening for sounds that aren't there anymore.

"What year is it?"

"Two thousand one." He frowns, watching the cellar door bang against the opening in the wind. "Where is everyone?"

I pull out my driver's license. I'd shoved it in my pocket since I refuse to carry a purse, much to Mary's disgust. "Here, look. It's 2018. You've been dead for a long, long time."

"I..." He trails off, staring at the date on my ID, horrified.

"You've been reliving this moment every day since then, but you don't have to anymore. All you have to do is step into the light and move on. People who love you are waiting for you."

Kane pops onto the roof beside me, startling both Steve and me. I hate when he does that.

"She's right, you know. I can take you through the light if you're afraid."

"I...who are you?"

"This is Kane. He's a reaper."

"Reaper?" Steve backs away from us, and I want to beat Kane. I almost had the kid into the light. Then Kane had to go scare the crap out of him.

"Easy, Steve." I keep my voice calm and very Officer Dan, like when he's trying to soothe me. "Kane is one of the good guys. It's his job to ferry lost souls to the other side, to where Jason is waiting for you."

"But...I...I can't be dead. It's not fair. I'm only sixteen...and Mark...oh, God, Mark. What about Mark?"

My heart breaks a little for him. He sounds so lost and forlorn. It's hard for some ghosts to accept they're dead, especially ones who died unexpectedly.

"I'm sorry, Steve, but you are dead. Mark isn't sixteen anymore. He's moved on, and it's time for you to do the same. Let Kane take you to Jason where you can be happy. There will be no fear or worry on the other side. You'll be loved and accepted and among family."

Kane holds out his hand. "It's going to be okay. I promise."

Steve eyeballs Kane's outstretched hand for the longest time before hesitantly placing his hand in the reaper's. "I…are you sure I'm dead?"

"I'm sure." Kane grips the teen's hand tighter. "But it's okay. Everything is going to be just fine. It's time to go."

Steve's face scrunches up, but he doesn't refuse. Instead, he follows the reaper into the glowing doorway that's standing open between this plane and the next. He gives me one more solemn look and steps into the light. The bright rip in the fabric of the planes closes behind them, and I let out a deep breath.

Steve was like most ghosts, shocked to learn they're dead, but at least it hadn't taken me hours to convince him. The last ghost I helped, I sat with her for over three hours trying to talk her into believing she was dead. I might actually get some stuff done today…crap.

I check my watch and start scrambling toward the ladder. I was supposed to pick Mary up fifteen minutes ago. She's going to kill me. Getting into my car, I take off for the Tulane campus, hoping she won't be too angry.

About The Author

So who am I? Well, I'm the crazy girl with an imagination that never shuts up. I LOVE scary movies. My friends laugh at me when I scare myself watching them and tell me to stop watching them, but who doesn't love to get scared? I grew up in a small town nestled in the southern mountains of West Virginia where I spent days roaming around in the woods, climbing trees, and causing general mayhem. Nights I would stay up reading Nancy Drew by flashlight under the covers until my parents yelled at me to go to sleep.

Growing up in a small town, I learned a lot of values and morals, I also learned parents have spies everywhere and there's always someone to tell your mama you were seen kissing a particular boy on a particular day just a little too long. So when you get grounded, what is there left to do? Read! My Aunt Jo gave me my first real romance novel. It was a romance titled "Lord Margrave's

Deception." I remember it fondly. But I also learned I had a deep and abiding love of mysteries and anything paranormal. As I grew up, I started to write just that and would entertain my friends with stories featuring them as main characters.

Now, I live Huntersville, NC where I entertain my niece and nephew and watch the cats get teased by the birds and laugh myself silly when they swoop down and then dive back up just out of reach. The cats start yelling something fierce…lol.

I love books, I love writing books, and I love entertaining people with my silly stories.

Facebook:
https://www.facebook.com/authorAprylBaker

Twitter:
https://twitter.com/AprylBaker

Website:
http://www.aprylbaker.com/

Bookbub:
https://www.bookbub.com/authors/apryl-baker

Wattpad:
http://www.wattpad.com/user/AprylBaker7

Newsletter:
https://www.aprylbaker.com/contact

Facebook Fan Page:
https://www.facebook.com/groups/AprylsAngel
s

Instagram:
https://www.instagram.com/apryl.baker

Blog:
https://www.mycrazycornerblog.com/

Amazon:
https://goo.gl/b1br13

Join our Reader Group on Facebook and don't miss out on meeting our authors and entering epic giveaways!

Join today! *"Where reading a book is your first step to becoming limitless..."*

https://www.facebook.com/groups/LimitlessReading/

Made in the USA
Monee, IL
20 October 2020